MR STRONGMOUSE
AND THE BABY

MOUSEMART
SUPERMARKET

SQUEAKY'S DISCO

FLUFFY BUT
GYM

For Molly and Maisie – H. O.

For Ellen and Megan – L. C.

ORCHARD BOOKS
338 Euston Road, London NW1 3BH
Orchard Books Australia
Level 17/207 Kent Street, Sydney, NSW 2000
First published in Great Britain in 2005
First paperback publication in 2006
This edition published in 2007 for Index Books Limited
ISBN 978 1 84362 588 9
Text © Hiawyn Oram 2005
Illustrations © Lynne Chapman 2005
The rights of Hiawyn Oram to be identified as the author
and Lynne Chapman to be identified as the illustrator
of this work have been asserted by them in accordance
with the Copyright, Designs and Patents Act, 1988.
A CIP catalogue record for this book is available
from the British Library.
1 3 5 7 9 10 8 6 4 2
Printed in Singapore
Orchard Books is a division of Hachette Children's Books

MR STRONGMOUSE
AND THE BABY

Hiawyn Oram & Lynne Chapman

ORCHARD BOOKS

Once there was a strong mouse.

He was this **strong**.

And this **strong**.

And this **strong!**

Then he started going
to the gym . . .

and got THIS strong.

FLUFFY
BUT FIRM
GYM

Mr Big of Big Fairgrounds saw
how strong he was and asked
him to become . . .

... the fairground's
Mr Strongmouse!

THE ONE & ONLY
MR STRONGMOUSE

He's Unbelievable!

Between the dodgems and dippers, Mr Showy of Showy TV saw how strong he was and asked him to become . . .

. . . the star of his own Strongmouse Series!

By now he could snap a tree trunk. **SNAP**

And lift a car.

But he'd grown so strong, he was too strong for his own good!

He pulled handles off doors,
doors off their hinges . . .

. . . and broke his own furniture
just mashing potato!

Wherever he went, whatever he did,
he caused crashings and collapsings.

chees
pop
eggs
more
Cheese

PIZZA

CHOC CHIP

PRICES TUMBLE
Kitchen roll packs—50p off!

He caused **shatterings** . . .

. . . and floodings.

And STILL each morning, he flexed his muscles in the mirror and said, "I am the strongest mouse in the world. I can do anything!"

And then one day, Mrs Petalsoft came flying out of her house next door crying, "Help! Mr Strongmouse! I've got to go out this very minute! It's an emergency . . .

". . . Will you take care of my baby?"

And the next thing, there he was - strongest mouse in the world - left in charge of a little baby!

"Yikes!" he cried. "I'd better tiptoe about quietly."

But could Mr Strongmouse tiptoe about quietly?

No, he could not.

WHAAAAAAA
went the baby.

KERRRASH!

"Whoops!" said Mr Strongmouse.

"You are so wide awake, I'd better
give you something nice to eat fast!"

But could Mr Strongmouse feed a baby fast?

"Whoops!" said Mr Strongmouse.
"You are so covered-in-green-stuff,
I'd better clean you up in a nice warm bath!"

But could
Mr Strongmouse
give a baby a nice
warm bath?

No, he could not!

WHAAAAAAAA
went the baby.

"Whaaaa! Whaaaa!"
said Mr Strongmouse.
"Seems that being strong
DOESN'T mean I can
do everything!"

"No, indeed," said Mrs Petalsoft,
coming home and surveying
the mess. "If you ask me,
Mr Strongmouse, you need
some lessons in being gentle."

"You're right! You're right," cried Mr Strongmouse. "I've got too strong for everybody's good. So, from now on I shall only use my strength to make myself useful!"

And that is . . .

. . . just what he did.

He also took Mrs Petalsoft's advice and enrolled in Softly-Does-It School . . .

. . . where he worked
so hard . . .

. . . he came top of his class,
proving once and for all,
you CAN be the strongest
mouse in the world . . .

. . . and still be

Mr Very Very Gentle!